I0705392

THE DEADLANDS
WINTER 2025

THE DEADLANDS

ISSUE 37, WINTER 2025

ISBN-13: 979-8-89116-011-8

psychopomp.com

Publisher: Sean Markey
Editor in Chief: E. Catherine Tobler
Poetry Editor: Nicasio Andres Reed
Social Media: Felicia Martínez
Art Director: inkshark
Nonfiction Editor: David Gilmore
Necromancer at Large: Amanda Downum
Copy Editor: Laura Blackwell
Copy Editor: Annika Barranti Klein
Designer: Christine M. Scott
Cover: "Au Crépuscule" by Erinthul

The Deadlands is distributed quarterly by:
    Psychopomp
    PO Box 36
    Woodbury, VT 05681

Subscriptions can be purchased at weightlessbooks.com. Individual issues can be obtained by joining our Patreon (with many deadly perks).
Join here: thedeadlands.com/patreon

WINTER 2025

TABLE OF CONTENTS

Fiction

EXTREME SPORTS CLUB
FOR OCTOGENARIANS

Kate Lechler

THERE'S SEVEN of them at the meet and greet, all eighty or older, clustered around the corner table at the Mellow Mushroom. The youngest person had her birthday three days ago: Jenny, a retired lawyer with a strawberry blonde bob that's silver at the roots. The rest have names like that, ending in *y*—Tiffany, Barry, Amy, and another Jenny. It's a Gen X thing. Only Dennis and Mark break the pattern. All but Dennis, who is Asian, are white. And all are ready to end their lives.

The Extreme Sports Club for Octogenarians (ESCO) was enfranchised a week after the Easy Passage Law was passed, legalizing self-directed death in the wake of new advances in longevity research. Don't have the money or desire to live forever? Enjoy a host of newly legal mortality options. Unfortunately, illicit drugs often had unanticipated side effects. Death cruises, with their nude balls and THC buffets, were garish and hedonistic; one-way space flights were prohibitively expensive. ESCO provided the pursuit of adventure and excitement, one last grand story to tell before, or while, biting the big one. Its tagline, "Die Awesome," is emblazoned in big letters on all the brochures that litter the table.

Lawyer-Jenny is used to assuming leadership positions, so she asks the question: "How do you want to die?"

"Hang gliding!" giggles Amy, then shields her mouth with her hand. "I'm a birder."

"Wrasslin' a gator." Barry thumps his chest with one meaty fist, priding himself on being the most in-shape guy at the table. "But the gator don't eat *me*. I die of a heart attack because I eat *it*."

"But alligator is a lean meat," the other Jenny, the one with the wig, says. Barry shrugs.

Bull running. Parachuting. White water rafting. All of their answers are predictable, except for one.

"Naked, on a hill, struck by lightning," Tiffany says, her voice high and childlike.

The first outing is wreck diving. Mark used to dream of swimming with great white sharks and, while it's not the time of year that they visit Florida's panhandle, he's excited by the possibility of any dangerous sea life.

They drop down one by one into water the color of a cloudy emerald. Almost indistinguishable in their gear, legs streamlined by flippers until everyone looks like mermaids. Even Tiffany, who walks with a cane, feels as active as a seal as she shoots down toward the wreck, which rises from the seabed like a jagged black tooth.

Frilled sponges flute up like vases. Wig-Jenny takes photos for her grandkids with an underwater camera. Dennis and Lawyer-Jenny explore the wheelhouse, where white anemones cluster so thickly, it is hard to see the pitted hull beneath. Fish dart in and out of windows and vents, and a slate-grey wolf eel flickers into a crevice, hovering just within reach of Barry's headlamp, its jutting jaws making it look like an ancient boxer. The beams of refracted light dip in and out of the water like fingers the sun is dabbling in a bowl.

On the other side of the ship, Mark waves to get everyone's attention. Where he's pointing, the hull seems to be collapsing, bubbling outward under some pressure. One rocky arm and then another unfurl, and finally everyone can see it for what it is—an octopus detaching from the side of the wreck, its color shifting as it moves. Mark claps his hands together soundlessly; through his faceplate, his eyes are wide and happy.

Everyone pairs off and starts surfacing, catching a strong current as they crest the hull, resting for two minutes at twenty feet, then again at ten. At this depth, the water looks hardly any color at all and the sun wobbles overhead. When they get to the surface, Lawyer-Jenny signals for the boat.

Only Mark has trouble ascending the ladder. The pilot of the boat helps haul him in, stretches his legs out on the deck, and peels off his mask. His skin is waxy, his face slack and peaceful.

"Is he breathing?" Wig-Jenny asks, her scalp gleaming beneath her thin cropped hair. "Check his pulse!"

The pilot checks. He's not breathing; his pulse is there, but thready.

"He came up too fast," Amy says, nodding. Her bun, secured with a crocheted scrunchie, flops on the top of her head. "Do CPR!"

"He's DNR," Dennis reminds her. "We all are."

"But...he just needs some air!" Amy's cousin almost drowned as a child. She remembers the thin stream of water he vomited after the lifeguard performed mouth-to-mouth.

"What do you think the point of this is?" Barry bellows, stripping halfway out of his wetsuit, the skin of his broad chest fish-pale in the daylight.

The six of them gather around while the pilot huddles over Mark, fingers on his throat every few minutes. It doesn't take long before the pilot stands, shakes his head, and returns to the helm.

They stand there, still dripping, clutching fingers, until Tiffany says, "He saw an octopus."

Everyone nods, repeating sadly, finally, "He saw an octopus."

By the time they make it back to shore, a coroner's van already waits.

The next outing is spelunking. Dennis brings his wife, whose badly dyed black hair sticks out wildly from her head at all angles.

"I love bats!" she says in lieu of introduction.

"This is my wife, JiYeon." Dennis slings an arm around her shoulder, kisses her cheek. "She loves bats."

The group's spirits are high in the wake of the loss of Mark the week before. Only Barry feels a little lost without his friend, the only other guy's guy in the group, although if he's honest with himself, it's just because Mark was tall. The rest take the diving expedition as proof that ESCO works, that they, too, can have an exciting death. Wig-Jenny tells everyone about the re-run of *Matlock* she watched the night before, as the cave guide points out different cave features.

"This is a curtain." The guide passes her light behind a rippling wall of mineral deposits, making it glow amber. "No touching, please," she says to Barry, who has reached out a hand. "The oils on your skin can damage the formations."

When she turns her back, Barry traces an M on the curtain, mouthing "Mark."

Ahead, the cave opens into a cavern, hung with what looks like patches of dark moss. Dennis points, grinning his perfect dentist's grin. "Myotis lucifugus!"

JiYeon gives an impromptu lecture on bats to Barry, Wig-Jenny, and Dennis, while Tiffany, Amy, and Lawyer-Jenny huddle next to a hump of rock at the mouth of the next passageway.

"I'm not afraid of them," Lawyer-Jenny says. "I just don't like their little hands."

Tiffany pats her back.

"Did you ever go to camp as a teenager?" Lawyer-Jenny changes the subject.

"That was the first time I got laid!" Tiffany says brightly. Amy coughs.

"You ever sing camp songs?" Lawyer-Jenny ticks off names of songs on her fingers: "Kumbaya," "Home on the Range," "Going on a Bear Hunt," "Hole in My Bucket…"

"Hole in My Bucket!"

Amy starts singing, a quavering alto. "There's a hole in my bucket, dear Liza, dear Liza…" The others join in, giggling.

"There's a hole in my bucket, dear Liza, a hole!" The walls of the cave dampen and echo their voices, until they sound like a choir stuck down a well.

When they get to the second Henry verse—"With straw, dear Henry, dear Henry…"—other voices join them. The group stands in a ragged circle, singing the rest of the song, while Barry backs them up with a "dum dum dum" in an ear-rattling bass. At the end, Tiffany lets out a sigh like she's just eaten a delicious meal, and the group laughs.

Half of the group is already out of the cave when a sharp cry comes from behind.

"Is everything okay?" Lawyer-Jenny pushes her way past Barry and Dennis, peering down into the entrance.

"It's okay," the guide calls. "She's sprained her ankle."

"It's broken." Wig-Jenny sobs. "I heard it crack."

Dennis climbs back into the cave, places fingers on her ankle, probing.

"You're a dentist, not a real doctor." Wig-Jenny continues to sob as a couple park rangers assist the cave guide in carrying her to a vehicle. The group gathers around the truck door to say their goodbyes before the ranger drives her away.

"The hell is she carrying on for?" Barry asks, while the truck rolls away. "I've broken plenty of bones in my time."

"That's it for her," Lawyer-Jenny—now the only Jenny—snaps. "A broken ankle, at her age? She won't be able to join us again."

———

Before the skydiving outing, the group welcomes a new member: Zeke Koran, a compact man with short brown hair and a beard.

"Can I ask how old you are?" Jenny says suspiciously.

"I'm thirty-eight," he smiles, then taps his chest. "I have terminal lung cancer. Was in remission for a while, but now it's back."

When they reach altitude, they can see the Gulf in the distance, shreds of cloud lacing the horizon. Below, the ground is a patchwork of green.

Barry goes first.

"Like a Band-Aid?" he jokes, then falls backward out of the plane. Against the backdrop of the ground, he looks like he is floating.

Amy, Tiffany, and Jenny approach Zeke.

"Can we go together?" Amy asks. "We want to make a star in the air, you know, holding hands?"

Zeke nods, and one by one they fall, maneuvering into a circle, grabbing hands, then swinging them in rhythm like they are skipping down the sidewalk together.

"Hoooo!" Zeke yells experimentally, to hear his own voice. Tiffany joins in, a long bellow, and Amy and Jenny begin hooting on their own.

"Fuck fuck fuck fuck fuck!" Amy says, shouting toward the plane. "I've always wanted to say that!" she yells.

They pull the tabs to deploy their parachutes and drift toward the ground. When the ground comes, it rushes them. They scramble for several steps, dragging chutes behind them.

Barry is already there, several yards away, staring into the sky and shielding his eyes from the sun. Jenny looks up, then gets the attention of the others, points overhead.

Two people, falling through the sky, holding hands, with no parachutes.

"Dennis and JiYeon," Tiffany says, feeling like she's swallowed the names.

The five of them track the couple with their eyes, willing their parachutes to deploy until they disappear, two specks, behind a line of trees bordering the field. Amy winces, bracing for a sound, but all they hear is vehicles from the airfield rushing past. The cloud of dust they stir hides everything in sight.

On the drive back, Barry stares out the window, wishing he'd thought of it first.

———

They don't meet for a couple weeks. When they do, it's back at the Mellow Mushroom where they first met.

"I still don't understand why I feel this way," Jenny says, picking at a pile of nachos.

Zeke sucks his teeth. "Maybe it was like a suicide pact. Dying together. Kinda romantic, no?" He twists a silver band around his finger.

Amy dabs at her eyes with a paper napkin and nods.

"Look, Big D just wanted to die awesome, not from something stupid like diabetes or heart failure." Barry doesn't look up from the menu when the waitress comes over, just orders the whiskey-glazed sliders.

"I never cared about dying awesome," Tiffany sniffs, her breathing finally under control. "What I really want is a beautiful death."

"What do you mean?" Zeke asks. There's no beautiful death for him. Lung cancer is painful and exhausting.

"I painted a picture once," she says dreamily, toying with the plastic umbrella in her drink, "when I was in my twenties, of a woman standing at the top of a hill, naked, arms stretched to the sky like a tree. She was being struck by lightning, but she was happy."

She looks around the table. "That's what I want. To die like that picture."

They go for a few more outings. Dirt biking. Horseback riding on treacherous mountain trails. Base jumping. Then one night Jenny calls them each to tell them that Tiffany's had a stroke.

They meet at 10:45 at Tiffany's house out in the suburbs, surrounded by lawn art. Giant moths and dragonflies made of twisted wire hang from a big oak and a bird bath in the center of her front yard is covered in shards of pottery.

Inside, Tiffany sits in a wheelchair near her television, which is showing a documentary about ants. Her face is tilted toward the television, her mouth twisted down on one side as though her skin is weighted with invisible ballast. The group huddles around her, no one sitting on the mismatched floral furniture. Amy is wearing bedroom slippers; Barry still has one ear-plug in. Only Zeke looks fully awake.

Tiffany mumbles something out of the side of her mouth, jerking her head toward the window.

Jenny and Amy shake their heads, uncomprehending, but Barry translates. "One last adventure."

They crowd out into the night, pack into Zeke's van, lifting Tiffany gently into the passenger seat and stowing her wheelchair in the back. For a while they just drive around Tallahassee in the dark. Zeke has the radio on, some loud eighties station—Elton John, then Queen.

"Bicycle, bicycle!" Barry sings loudly, and after a few repetitions, everyone joins in. They stop at Dairy Queen and everyone orders a different flavor of Blizzard and shares bites across the back of the bench seats.

It starts to rain and the air turns silver. Their conversation dulls as everyone listens to the thunder, watching the lightning glow behind distant clouds.

"A big storm," Amy says, and everyone nods.

Tiffany says something, but Zeke can't quite make it out at first. "What's that?"

"The hilllll," she says again, elongating each word so as to be understood. "The one. From mmmy paintinnnng."

The radio deejay announces another song, and Tiffany reaches laboriously under her chair to pull out an umbrella, brandishing it for a moment with one hand like a sword.

"Take me," she says.

Zeke slows the van down, pulls off on the shoulder of the two-lane road. He keeps his hands at ten and two while he says, softly, "Honey…the likelihood is that you'll just get sick. You'll get cold and wet and get pneumonia."

"Don't," Tiffany grinds out, fixing him with a stare. "Don't. Call meeee. Honey."

Jenny leans forward from her position in the middle of the bench seat and puts a hand on Tiffany's arm. Tiffany's shaking underneath her windbreaker, and she doesn't bother trying to turn toward Jenny. She just nods again, harder, and Jenny responds with a squeeze.

"Take us there, Zeke."

They take a few detours, because Tiffany isn't exactly sure where this hill is. But then Amy looks on her phone. "There's a page here about it, they say that lightning has struck there 120 times in the last five years. Is this it?" She pushes the enlarged text into Tiffany's face, who nods.

When they arrive, no one else is around. They park the van on the gravel road, then push Tiffany's chair through the wet pebbles. Near the top of the hill is a pine tree, but the ground is actually sloped from the tree, coming to a point, an exposed bald with a few rocks in outline against the storm.

"Is this going to work?" Barry's voice sounds uncharacteristically doubtful as he huffs.

Jenny slips a little in the gravel. "Hey, asshole, get over here and help," she yells at Barry. He blusters a bit, but takes a handle of the wheelchair from Jenny.

When they reach the tree, Zeke and Barry stop with Tiffany under its branches. She turns on her flashlight, aims it at her face, then giggles.

"We're all scared enough as it is," Amy says, impatient. "So now what?"

Tiffany shines her light up the hill, the top of which is a dozen feet above the ground where they now stand.

Zeke and Barry grunt, trying to roll the chair the last few steep feet of the hill. The wheels keep getting stuck in the mud, though, so Zeke lifts Tiffany out, cradling her in his arms, while Barry and Jenny walk the chair to the crest. Once there, Zeke sits Tiffany back in her chair, tucking the edges of her jacket tighter around her.

"You got your umbrella?" he says.

She lifts it into the air and he flinches, then laughs. "Not yet, Tiff!"

She grins into the flashlight. "I'm rrrready." She pats her pocket. "My phone."

They nod, half-sliding down the hill, and make their way back to the van. They open the back doors, facing the hill, and kneel on the bench seats, still listening to the radio in silence.

"It's about to get bad," Zeke says, holding his phone with the Doppler map highlighted in reds and yellows. "Should we close those doors?"

"No way," Jenny says stalwartly.

The rain pounds the earth, bouncing to shower the back seat of the van with spray. It makes the air gray, almost opaque. But now and then lightning flashes above, outlining the clouds in electric white and lighting them from within as if they were lanterns. When this happens, they see Tiffany, holding the umbrella as high as she can, the flashlight still trained on her face, her white hair, her soaked nightgown.

Flashes come faster and faster, the time between the flash and rumble decreasing. The ground shakes after a giant crack and Amy gasps.

"Behind us," Jenny says, patting Amy on the shoulder.

The lighting seems to be directly overhead now, crackling in waves within the masses of clouds that made them seem alive, nuclear, like the face of God hidden from Moses, hidden in the burning bush.

One finger of lightning reaches down, almost touching the tree, before splintering and dissipating. But the clouds overhead are incandescent. And Tiffany's light moves.

"What's she doing?" Barry asks. "Standing?"

Another crash, overhead, and they see her, standing stoop shouldered in front of her chair, stabilizing herself with one hand on the arm and the other reaching high in the sky, lifting her umbrella. Her wet hair gleams, plastered to her scalp and her neck, and she smiles, face turned to the sky.

Another crash, and she's lifted her hand from the handle of the chair, stretched it out to the sky as if in supplication.

When it comes, it's a rip in the sky. It hits Tiffany's umbrella, which goes up in a flash of flames, polyester burning so fast there's no chance there'll be anything left.

She stands, paralyzed, stiff, her spine almost perfectly straight, her head thrown back, a halo of light surrounding her, limning her clothing, her chair. Nothing else is on fire except for the umbrella, but the arm holding the umbrella is struck rigid, coursing with electricity, each muscle locked. Which means that her smile is locked, too, her eyes fixed on the sky as it bends down to embrace her.

Zeke whoops. Jenny and Amy gulp and bite their lips in the same expression.

"That's how I'd like to go," Barry sighs.

Poetry

THE RIVER

Zaynab Iliyasu Bobi

for the women widowed by boko haram

i will tell you about the mother of three & the children she hasn't lost, yet. keep the count, because what is lost will always find a way to remain lost. remember, she hasn't lost them yet. one of the son's mouths hasn't been purged by the bullet to cough out blood. & the river is far away from where i stand to write this poem. let's do a bit of retelling. i will start from the beginning. i promise no one will be lost. what is lost remains lost. the river. no one knows the aches of the mother like the river. but before the river, there was a home. just like Warsan said, no one leaves home unless home is the mouth of a shark. God, i hate quietness, said the loud cries from guns. i know you will be wondering about the husband. don't worry yet, what is lost remains lost. instead, worry about the crystals in her sons' eyes before they were clouded by fear. back to her husband. you would find her head-tie on his face. there was a downfall & the sons witnessed it, too. that is all i can tell you because what is lost remains lost. there are things you would come to learn about the mother that might seem wrong, but remember what is lost remains lost. instead, imagine you are standing by the riverbed & the mother is standing, too. & there is another woman beside her breastfeeding the child she would later throw into the river. don't call it cruelty. remember, what is lost remains lost & a mother knows all about love & its burden.

Fiction

HIS LOVE'S ASHES ON HIS TONGUE

Monte Lin

INCENSE FOGGED UP the Food District—not the official name, a moniker only because of the food stalls, including Hui selling her pig's blood cake. Even though the ersatz pig was from protein growth tanks and the blood not exactly blood but leftover protein nutrient baths. Instead of the light pink, mildly red of actual pig's blood cake, Hui's dishes had a dark red, almost black color. A bit of garlic, some chives and radish, and ridiculously expensive rice, and Gabriel felt right at home.

Save for the thick nitrogen atmosphere overhead and the looming walls of the caldera.

Necropolis sat in the crater of a caldera, creating a natural bubble to capture the thin oxygen, some from the initial reclamation with carbon dioxide scrubbers, others from the gene-mod bamboo growing in wild, chaotic, clustered patches. Geothermal piping provided some heat, but everyone wore heat-insulated jackets. Everyone also carried blood oxygenator injectors like gold, except gold was non-existent here, too much mass to carry on a ship and not important enough to exclusively mine for.

"Do you have tea?" Gabriel asked.

"Too expensive this time around." Hui shook her head. She avoided looking directly in his eyes. "How many?"

"A hundred and six days."

Hui now looked directly at Gabriel, giving an expression he recognized, a look she gave all the old timers, the ones hitting a couple hundred, three hundred-plus days. A look of pity, sympathy, but also a "WTF is wrong with you" look. An auntie look. A look reserved for memory-eaters.

A smattering of travelers coming to Necropolis are rich tourists or funding-starved archeologists, those with the means to stay and explore the city. The rest bring the ashes of their dead in hopes the city can help them commune with their memory. A lucky few do find some catharsis. Most leave disappointed. Some stay, delving into one memory or another, getting lost more and more. Memory-eaters.

Before they get called memory-eaters, the people who arrive in Necropolis call themselves pilgrims. Each carry their loved one's ashes in a small container: pendants, lightweight polymer spheres or cubes, small urns. Like all of the other pilgrims, Gabriel had stood disappointed on the landing pad, looking out over the caldera, a wasteland with sulfuric steam lazily wisping up the caldera walls. (Necropolis orbits close enough to the rogue ice giant Hades that its gravity causes only mild volcanic activity, good for geothermal power with the occasional earthquake.) Following the trail of mourners, pausing to inject some oxygen, Gabriel swore he could smell a dry, acrid, perpetually autumnal air, while keeping an eye on the pale, red light strips on both sides of the well-worn path.

People clustered ahead, and he welcomed the rest. Some people sat on the ground, others bent over, breathing heavily, heads down and hands on knees. When he finally reached the cluster, he saw them all touching a column of some lighter-colored concrete-like material, embedded in the volcanic stone. Everyone had removed their gloves. He could see shapes and patterns on the column, worn down by weather or by human hands, Gabriel couldn't tell.

When he placed an ungloved hand onto the column, he
feels the strong fingers of his hand wrap around his tiny one, crushing his phalanges in an awkward way as he pulls him across the field away from the others as the sharp, orange scent of freshly cut grass bites at his olfactory organs and his ambulatory limbs stumble over his loose bindings even as he cries, "Please, I'm sorry, father!"

Gabriel pulled away and stumbled, falling to the ground, as the other pilgrims stood or sat or laid transfixed in memories. Those who hadn't touched the wall helped him up, but they all asked, "What did you see? Who did you see? Is it true?"

"My father…no, *a* father…"

The pilgrims gasped and most rushed to touch the column but a few grabbed Gabriel, not to help him up, but to take part in his vision. The crowding, the pushing, the shoving, the shouting…too much commotion and not enough breathing, and for Gabriel it all went dark.

Gabriel had woken up in a first aid tent, halfway between the landing pad and the column. He had not noticed it when he walked past, as he kept his gaze down on the red-light strips. The people here weren't medical doctors, mostly flight personnel with first aid experience. They had oxygen injectors, but also the tent was pressurized with oxygen.

Panic tightened around his heart and he patted himself and the cot he lay on. His vision turned red as he hyperventilated. The medic handed him the urn and leaned close with an injector. Gabriel pulled the urn tight to his chest and shook his head.

"I'm fine. I'm fine."

Danny was the one who held him when he panicked: over Gabriel's layoff, when the gestation procedures failed, when he had that health scare that eventually turned out to be nothing. ("See? We're going to live together, forever," Danny had said.) Gabriel always felt guilt over the fact that Danny had suffered too, but he just didn't seem to show it.

From the medic, he learned the column, the Father Stone, had a gao memory of their father, but weathering, time, or constant human contact had weakened the memory property of the stone. Most felt nothing, a few a vague sensation of disappointment (though whether theirs or from the memory, no one can say definitively), and only a few, like Gabriel, got a full memory.

And he didn't even want it.

He also learned the basic layout of Necropolis. Astrocartographers tried to name the rogue ice giant Mnemosyne. Archeologists called it Gaohome, but who cares what eggheads think? Several corporations had bought, renamed, and rebranded the planet, but when its import was the dead and its only exports memories and grief, the name Hades stuck.

And then you had Necropolis, one of Hades's moons, its eponymous settlement divided into districts. The Food District had tent encampments and the food stalls, and was where most people buried their dead. The Water District had the human water reclamation systems and geothermal pumps.

But the Spirit District had the powerful, surreal memories: strange sensations and truly alien thoughts, of high concepts, ideas, bits of gao history. Archeologists and engineers lurked there. Rumors of drug users and sellers too. There were other rumors that someone had an alcohol still, but grain was too valuable to waste as alcohol. People who went there came back changed or wrong, including the scientists. The majority of the Spirit District population were the memory-eaters, bathing in the years, decades, maybe centuries of gao memories.

The medic shook her head and told Gabriel to bury his husband and get out. "Don't become a memory-eater. Alien memories will just eat up your mind, over time."

Whether the gao implanted their memory stones here as an archive or as a cemetery, no one could say yet. Some scientists thought the gao had made this moon a kind of amusement park. Only humans thought this place holy.

Walking into the Food District proper, he found that same concrete-like stone, shaped in statuary and architecture short enough to lie or sit on, like a commercial park in a busy city, but built into the earth, the side of the caldera crater. He found pilgrims lounging on the structures, contorting as if dreaming, eyes open and staring at nothing, sometimes whispering or shouting or weeping at a gao memory they mistook for their own. Trinkets with ashes in the center, urns, and small shrines decorated the whole space, a massive, makeshift columbarium. When Gabriel sat down, he

gasps for air as the current pulls him down again and this time some water gets into his breathing orifice causing him to cough out much needed air and the rising panic spreads to his appendages as they lash out at the water yet it does not let him go and he feels the fluids rush into his oxygenation organ threatening to dilute the blood pool and all he needs to do is find some solid land some anchor

It took all his will to pull away from the memory, his arms holding Danny's urn so tight he bruised his ribs. Taking deep breaths in the oxygen-thin atmosphere did not calm his racing heart. Instead, the pain from the injector on the side of his neck provided the same stim.

Gabriel reminded himself he hadn't come here to experience another being's memories. He came here to reconcile his own.

The memory-eaters claimed truth seekers didn't stay in the Food District for very long. The memories were too concrete, too obviously not-yours. Too real. Too gao. Memory-eaters looked for that soul-crushing loss, that gut-wrenching emptiness, the disturbing weirdness. The more crushing, the more weird, the better.

How did the gao mourn their dead? And in knowing, could it help us grieve?

A few tried the Water District only to get in trouble with the grumpy engineers. Memory-eaters weren't looking for trouble or rational arguments about their safety, otherwise they'd have never come to Necropolis. They were still pilgrims, just a different kind.

Gabriel didn't know what he was anymore. He clutched his polymer urn to his chest. As he feared, the memories of the

Food District hadn't given him any answers. Danny remained cold ash in the urn and not vibrant and alive. The urn was too small to fit in the hole in his heart. He needed to go deeper.

He smelled no incense here in the Spirit, a sign this wasn't a place for honoring the dead but to find them in katabasis, like the tale of the buddha searching the hells for his mother. No one had put up any lights along the path here, and so Gabriel stumbled across comatose bodies on the floor, his hand-held light glowing a faint red. Someone offered him what looked to be an oxygen injector and he declined, then realized it was for drugs. He already knew the names for the different varieties, from soft to harsh, from depressants to stimulants, hallucinogens to enhancements.

A stone sculpture shaped vaguely like a chair had no occupant, so Gabriel set his urn down on one of the "arms," sat down, and pressed his hands onto the cold stone

a mating ball of lovers press their bodies against each other grabbing at appendages and touching exposed sweaty skin angrily stumbling to the floor as the sun turns dim bathing them in purple shadows highlighting by the infrared lights of the street and the bitter scent of dust mixes with the dizzying scent of desire

The sensations almost made him vomit. He couldn't help but stumble to another empty section to plunge his hand into the stone, cracking his knuckles and hurting his fingers

coiled together scales rubbing against scales skin shedding in relief from the nonstop itchiness under a warm sun and the warm sand sliding underneath and the comfortable weight of the rodent in your belly slowly dissolving but your companion is starving having been less lucky their scales dry and scarred

more, he needed more, there had to be an answer, it can't all be nonsense

laying your skull down in the roots of a tree to return to where you came from the dirt in your eyes stones in your mouth

A memory-eater lifted up an injector and said, "For nausea," and this time Gabriel agreed. It was also a familiar relaxant and an invitation as probing hands reached for him, sliding between his jacket and his heat cycle shirt. In a moment, he melted into the touch, thinking, remembering, re-remembering, experiencing, and re-experiencing until he became that slurry of lust, comfort, death, surrender, loneliness.

These were the things of poets, but before he completely succumbed, Gabriel thought this planet should belong to the epic, historical novelists.

———

He had been here before. Not Necropolis, but the liminal, numbed nothingness of a drug stupor. His family had put him under after Danny died, supposedly for his own good. The funeral, the storing of their possessions, the closing of his rental account, his hospital stay—all melted into each other. The anti-panic drugs made time float on by, a blur of eating, pissing, shitting, and sleeping.

And then he was "cured," as the doctors proclaimed, or more likely, the treatment costs and hassle got too onerous for his family. He returned home with a prescription of drugs.

Maybe those were placebos or generics, but he came out of the haze long enough to overhear his family talk about Danny's ashes:

"We really need to inter this thing."

"Gabe should be doing that."

"You think he's going to be able to do that?"

"We have a nice columbarium by the family plot."

"Gabe should choose where Danny is put."

"It's only temporary. He can be reburied later."

That night, Gabriel packed up a few clothes, Danny's urn, and the remaining drugs. He walked out the door and shipped himself to Necropolis.

———

"How long have you been here?" Gabriel asked.

"A thousand four hundred and thirty-six days," said the memory-eater, almost with pride.

It wasn't the number that brought Gabriel out of the slurry. Who knows how many days he had been here since the drugs and memories had dampened his hunger, but he felt desiccated, drained, dried up like Earth's old tree leaves.

It was the last memory he touched that did it

coiled around the support bar they can't understand the why of it their eyes narrow to slits and out the side ship window the fading sun's light resolves the asteroid tumbling in the emptiness they reach out with their phalanges to try to catch the ever-shrinking rock and all they can think of is the endless cold empty nothingness those inside will face forever and ever and ever and ever and ever

Nothing like the adrenaline rush of panic to shake off a stupor and then tears to clear the heart and head. He held on to the urn for as long as the sobs continued, and when they stopped it was as if his chest had opened like a flower in a newly emerging sun that Hades will never see.

Danny never considered where he'd be buried: "I'd be dead, so what would I care?" He had no family plot, no family beyond Gabriel, and life was what concerned him. But Gabriel couldn't believe that he should scatter Danny to the stars or dump him in a pit in a random cemetery.

What did Danny want?

Danny would probably never have come here. It was Gabriel who knew the actual name of the moon (Acheron), who had read all the papers about the gao and the memory stones. Gabriel read the false rumors about the memory-eaters, how the stones changed their genetics, that the gao reproduced through these stones. Danny called that "xenophobic nonsense" and Gabriel stuffed the fascination down deep, unwilling to admit he wanted to travel to a rogue planet out in the middle of empty space between Earth and the Centauri system.

No, Danny would have appreciated this moon. But in his own way. He'd see the people making pig's blood cake, the medics volunteering at the tent, even the memory-eaters undulating down below as if they were snakes, and remark on how weird *humans* were.

The air was moist and sticky, the walls of the caverns slick and dripping. Gabriel heard the shallow breathing, the air rushing past in gulps, the floor and walls exhaling and inhaling, but was that the sound of the memory-eaters or the water reclamation and purification pumps?

The memory-eaters all clung to him weakly as he got up, grabbed the urn, and stumbled away. Their arms extended in the air left an image of desperation, the willingness to interpret the memories how they wanted, a bit too space hippie. He needed something more concrete, he needed food, he needed real sleep.

———

He had assumed Danny would be there always. Just one more year of work. Save more money. Flights back to Titan too expensive. Just another year. With life extensions, they should have had all the time in the galaxy to explore other worlds. Except, shuttle accident.

There was a possibility that the ashes in the urn contained shuttle.

There was a possibility that the ashes also had space dust.

An irony or poetic metaphor for an astro-engineer?

Gabriel had a mild headache, perhaps from coming off of the recreational drugs, perhaps due to low oxygen, so he rented an oxygenated chamber and purchased a sleeping bag for an outrageous amount. (Now he realized why pilgrims insisted on bringing camping supplies.)

The chamber was heated. Without embarrassment, he took off his dirty clothing to change in front of everyone. No one looked or glared or stared. Grief had pulled everyone within.

The chamber dripped with condensation, the geothermal heating and the aquifer giving rise to escaped steam. He found a driest-as-possible spot. He picked up the urn

a nanowire blade thinned by determination can solve this difficult problem

his hand went slack but he caught the urn in his other hand

a heart stilled against a thunder of engines lets me maintain some armor for the mind

he placed both hands on the urn

proton and antiproton annihilation and creation -1 + 1 = 0 but never true the loss is always greater than the fill leaving the community diminished

how could this polymer urn have memories like a gao stone?

empty space is more than an absence but the promise it will be filled with time

yes, this was what he had been looking for

becoming a quantum state a particle with discreet boundaries but a waveform merging with another the frequency increasing or becoming complex

this was Danny

The funeral urn remembered. Can a thing "re-member," if the memory was new? And did the urn itself remember or did the ashes contain the memory? Gabriel could not bring himself to answer this question by opening the urn to touch the remains. He had a momentary image of ashes on his tongue. (And ashes was a misnomer, since they were really pulverized bones.)

Instead, he held onto the urn

feeling the brush of stubble on Danny's face against his own. Rough, scratchy, but like running your bare feet on warm carpet. Danny mutters, "Gabe, I just need a few minutes," turning his head one way or the other, but does nothing to prevent Gabe from rubbing his cheek against his stubble.

Gabe lies against Danny's warm and comforting chest, while his husband has one arm up holding the screen, thumb flicking up and down to read technical papers, the other arm wrapped around Gabe. This is Danny, lightly scolding, his mind always on something else, but his free arm around him, holding him firm, never complaining.

Danny kisses Gabe on the top of his head and says, "Okay, okay. I'm done reading. What did you want to do today?"

———

Gabriel slept. Since Necropolis had no sun, the lights stayed on, and people worked all hours; there was no physical way to tell time, only local chronometers. He hadn't checked the time before he had fallen asleep. Maybe a whole Earth day's worth?

Hungry again. He headed back to the Food District, and Hui was there once more, chopping the blood cake into cubes. She caught his eye and paused. She still asked, "How many?" but a bit slower, as if she wasn't sure she should ask.

"Too many."

Hui paused, looked deeper into Gabriel's eyes. He realized that this wasn't a look of pity, maybe never was a look of pity, but of understanding. Of being exhausted from a long journey.

"Sit. Eat."

She served him a bowl of the blood cake, radish, onions, chives, and rice. He tore into it, shoveling chopstick-scoops full into his mouth. He set the bowl down to breathe and saw a cup of dark red steaming tea in front of him.

"Where did you get that?!"

Hui shushed him, reached across the booth to lightly slap at his head, missing skull but catching a little bit of hair. "Don't make a fuss. A secret stash. For finally waking up. You need to clear that messy head of yours."

The cup took a little time to cool, or Gabriel's fingers took a little time to warm up to match temperatures, before he could take a sip. It had a bitter, burnt taste, stronger than he expected but fainter than it should. The leaves must have been old. But it unclenched another flower in his head. He had a decision to make.

"Have you heard of human-made things gaining memories?"

Hui paused and then nodded near-imperceptibly. "It usually means the memory-eater has been here too long. Maybe they have become more gao than human."

"What happens if you take a piece of Necropolis with you? Does it keep the memories?"

Hui shrugged. "The archeologists haven't been able to bring a piece back. Maybe because it's gao not human. Maybe there is a gao battery that powers the stones. But that doesn't stop people from chipping away at a stone, erasing memories for their own selfish reasons. Pretty soon there won't be anything gao left but rubble."

"But does it keep the memory?"

Hui shrugged again. "They don't come back to tell us."

"Why are you here, Hui?"

She nodded, as if expecting the question. "I buried my husband here. Then I became a memory-eater. I came out and saw I was done grieving, but I also didn't have anywhere else to go." She leaned close. "This tea was the first thing I tasted after I came out of there."

"Aren't we supposed to bury our loved ones back home?"

"This was a home, a Gaohome, home for the gao. Humans were the ones who named this planet after a god of the dead and this moon after a river of sorrow. As if death and re-memory was something to bury and not cherish."

This time, Gabriel wore gloves. He held the urn in both hands. In the Spirit District, he walked up to the archeologists and asked, "I heard you have a columbarium here?"

They nodded and took him to a chamber. This one was old, the edges of the walls worn down, the floor carved by thousands of long-dead appendages etching away at the stone. He saw hundreds of crèches all filled with containers of all shapes and sizes, simple cylinders, swirls, bottles of some kind, on and on. These were all covered in dust. Gao remains. Gao re-memories.

The archeologists brought him to where the crèches were mostly empty, and here he recognized human-made urns of black polymer. There were only a few, barely a dozen. And one with the face of the smiling buddha. Hui's husband.

"All of these people don't have homes to be buried at," one of the archeologists said. "Seems a shame to send mourners away. Besides, we cleared this area already and everyone who asked has been respectful. We think the gao would want more memories here to keep this place alive."

Gabriel picked a crèche next to Hui's husband. Danny wouldn't want to be separated from people. He felt other people were his home, so it seemed fitting. Gabriel placed the urn carefully in the crèche and it almost sank into the space, wanting to be there.

"Most people say some last, parting words. I can give you some privacy."

"It's okay. He remembers what I want to say."

SUFFER THE BLESSING

Aaron Knuckey

Mother always said her Bible was a cage she kept closed so God couldn't get out.

When she died I opened it

and the living room metamorphosed: gaudy wallpaper clouds blossomed outwards and floated away, the bells of apocalyptic trumpets sprouted from floorboards like brass mushrooms, paperbacks became scrolls scabbed over with seals.

> *Come and see prophecies revealed as promises.*
> *Come and see the foundations laid for the New Kingdom.*
> *Come and see...*

-"Cassandra, if there's something you want to share with the whole class please raise your hand."
-"I'm sorry, Mrs. Baumgartner. But the angels emerging in our woodshed all have scythe blades for wings. When they sing, their hymns are the secrets the moon whispers back to the wolves. I haven't been able to sleep. Can you come over? Can you see?"
-"Cassandra, if I need to contact your father..."

...who is genuflecting before the flaming gate that was once a TV? He won't answer. But what does he glimpse within? It's too bright for me to look. Will we have to walk into that silver-gold fire hand in hand one day? Will Father comfort me or will I comfort him? What can any of us know of each other before the burning is born? And borne?

Mother, the house is rotting into Heaven.

Mother, you still aren't here.

Mother, if anything truly dwelt in your Good Book it was just a virus wearing a King James mask, and I can close that heavy leather cover but I can never scrape the holy infection from the red coral of my mind so instead I must imagine a divinity worthy of your love and then place you in its eternal arms instead,

meaning somewhere above the cosmos you embrace yourself.

Nonfiction

FIVE TREASURED TROPES OF SFF K-DRAMAS

Cressida Blake Roe

MANY WELL-RESPECTED Korean television dramas of the past decade have been in the realm of SFFH, firmly establishing the speculative and slipstream as mainstays of the form, whether as the primary genre of the show or to enliven or mystify a more grounded plot. Over time, this K-drama genre has evolved its own vernacular of tropes, imagery, and plot points that shows return to again and again in exploration and execution of the stories they want to tell. Here are five essential features.

GODS, PSYCHOPOMPS, AND OTHER SUPERNATURAL BEINGS

Perhaps the most quintessential speculative K-drama protagonist is the titular dokkaebi, or goblin, from tvN's *Goblin* (aka *Guardian: The Lonely and Great God*; 2016–2017). Brought back to life after a selfish death, the goblin Kim Shin needs to learn a lesson about the value of human love and compassion by finding his bride and using his immortality for good, a common character arc for the genre's supernatural protagonists. Some such characters, like the dokkaebi and the gumiho (the nine-tailed fox) are borrowed from Korean folklore, but many others are recognizable from Western literature, religion, and mythology, such as angels of doom, aliens from other stars, mermaids, and vampires. Whether from East or West, nonhuman protagonists are often framed against their mortal love interests to explore overarching questions about moral action, empathy, and the difficult choices demanded of a short and fragile life. On a lighter side, they're often called upon to blend in with society and hide their powerful natures, leading to amusing mishaps as they learn how to behave according to social mores and cope with modern technology. Speculative shows that also lean into horror, such as *Sweet Home* (2020–2024) and *Parasyte: The Grey* (2024), feature hybrid supernatural characters as a way to subvert this mortal/monstrous binary and illustrate the ambiguity of human impulses.

DEALINGS WITH DEATH

Perhaps not unsurprisingly in stories with a strong stake in immortality, the presence of Death and the afterlife emerges as a counterpoint, either with a claim on an important human character or as a means to ask big questions about coping with impermanence and mortality. Death either comes personified as an underworld deity, when the story needs a source of power, or as a more relatable psychopomp-like figure, sometimes with a human history that can provide speculation on life's mysteries and their appeal from a place of distance. Some prominent characters connected to death include *Goblin*'s fan-favorite grim reaper, Wang Yeo, seeking for the sin that traps him in this work; Jang Man-Wol of *Hotel del Luna* (2019), who sets up a halfway hotel to help ghosts finish their earthly business; Taluipa from *The Tale of the Nine Tailed* (2020) and its sequel (2023), the bureaucratic regulator of afterlife immigration; or the crisis management psychopomps of *Tomorrow* (2022), who must prevent untimely deaths as much as facilitate them. While some earlier dramas focus on death and eternality as a contrast to the natural brevity of human lives, more recent shows, such as *Tomorrow* and *Death's Game* (2023), have used this theme to talk about suicide, as self-harm and suicide are social crises troubling many young people in Korea, and to show the importance of holding on to life in the face of its obstacles.

MANY LIFETIMES

On the other side of this deathly theme is that of reincarnation and a soul's journey across lifetimes. Both supernatural and mortal characters can experience multiple lifetimes, either over the course of the show or simply included in their backstory as an origin point for present conflicts. Reincarnation comes from Buddhist belief, where the cycle of rebirth is necessary to work through karma and attain liberation, though the shows don't always—or even often—reference these religious roots. Rather, reincarnation serves as a means to tie characters together across the differing situations of historical periods with humorous, as in *From Now On, Showtime!* (2022), or tragic, as in *Chicago Typewriter* (2017), consequences. Reincarnation also plays a large part in the love and hate stories of these dramas: Lee Yeon, the immortal gumiho in *The Tale of the Nine Tailed*, waits several hundred years for the reincarnation of his first love, whose death he was responsible for. *Goblin*'s Kim Shin and Wang Yeo must resolve the enmity of their past lives to cut themselves free from the bitterness holding them back from Heaven. Finally, those caught between lives, such as ghosts, spirits, and zombies, also feature frequently as side characters, sometimes as a bridge for human characters to reach the supernatural world or as a deathless antagonistic force.

TIME TRAVEL

Reincarnation isn't the only means through which a K-drama plot can move around in time, however. Time travel broadens the definition of an SFF show, as it can introduce a speculative or magical flavor to an otherwise realistic plotline and suggest a necessary suspension of disbelief to follow the story to its close. Some dramas use it as a jumping-off point for saeguk period dramas by introducing a modern character, such as Go Ha-Jin in *Moon Lovers: Scarlet Heart Ryeo* (2016) and Jang Bong-Hwan in *Mr. Queen* (2020–2021), into a historical setting, where they become involved in political schemes and struggle to adapt to their new circumstances. Other dramas use time travel to give their protagonists second chances, establishing an initial situation that ends, as in the case of *Again My Life* (2022), *Reborn Rich* (2022), and *Lovely Runner* (2024), in a major character's death. Offered a miraculous chance for a do-over, the protagonist can travel to the past with the memories of their original timeline intact to solve mysteries, plot revenge, and generally redirect circumstances to create a happier future. Through these devices, time travel plots often involve the closest thing to what SFF K-dramas have of magic, as the means of the time travel is typically hand-waved and vague. Only a few shows explicitly use a time machine or center a character whose ability to time travel precedes the inciting events of the plot.

FATE

Finally, fate casts a long shadow across all K-dramas. While grand conversations about fate can come across as a flimsy yet convenient reason for a main couple to end up together, the notion itself possesses a deeper philosophical origin. "Inyeon" or "unmyeong" in Korean, this definition of fate arises from a Buddhist notion that all human connections are predestined or divinely ordained, responsible not only for the multi-lifetime approach to love stories, but also for the deeply explored relationships among secondary characters that K-dramas are so renowned for. Fate sometimes takes an active role in the plot—personified in *Goblin* as God, speaking to the protagonists about the direction their lives must take—though more often it remains abstract, a concept that guides characters through choices or leads them to accept difficult circumstances, including important sacrifices. Furthermore, it doesn't contradict free will or mean that people are robbed of personal agency: as the voice of God states in *Goblin*, "Fate is a question I ask someone. The answer is something you must find for yourselves." The message that meaningful personal connection is often the answer is a strong statement to these shows' priorities and overall message.

ASK A NECROMANCER:
THE AUTOPSY OF A HORROR FILM

Amanda Downum

IT MAY COME as no surprise that ever since I was a wee ghoul, I've loved horror films. My knowledge is nowhere near encyclopedic, but back in the ancient days of the video store, I spent hours and hours haunting the horror section looking for new monsters to fall in love with. In the past several years I've dropped farther and farther behind on new releases, but I still want to fall in love.

An unfortunate side effect of writing fiction professionally was that I've become incredibly fussy about prose. An unfortunate side effect of being elbow-deep in dead bodies is that I've become unbearable to watch movies with. I've turned into one of those people with specialized knowledge who can't keep their opinions to themselves. (For some people it's horses, or guns, or historical clothing; for me, it's corpses.)

Usually the question I get when people find out my profession is, did I watch *Six Feet Under?* (Only a few episodes.) More recently, however, people have been asking if I've seen *The Autopsy of Jane Doe.* So many people, in fact, that I finally sat down with my long-suffering partner and turned it on. And now you, beloved readers, can suffer as well.

Obviously this will contain spoilers for the film. Proceed with caution.

We open with police investigating a murder scene in Grantham, Virginia. While searching the house, the police discover the unaccounted for—and by all appearances, very fresh—dead body of a young woman half-buried in the base-ment.

Body in the basement, I know, I know, it's serious…

The mystery corpse bothers the sheriff far more than the violent murders of people he knew, so they bundle our titular Jane Doe up and deliver her to the…

Morgue and Crematorium? A family-owned morgue and crematorium? Is this a Virginia thing? Funeral homes with crematories are perfectly normal, but I have never seen a family-owned morgue, or a morgue that advertised as such. At the basic definition, a morgue is a place where bodies are stored. Hospital morgues hold bodies until a funeral home picks them up for the family. (Usually no longer than 72 hours, and they don't want to hold them that long.) If a coroner or medical examiner requests an autopsy, the body will go to a municipal or county morgue.

What's the difference between a coroner and a medical examiner? I'm so glad you asked! A medical examiner has a medical degree, usually with specialized training in pathol-ogy. A coroner is an elected or appointed position. You can be a judge, a farmer, a mystery writer, or just about anything and be elected coroner. Many coroners do have some medical training, especially in larger cities, but in some areas no expe-rience whatsoever is required for the office. Depending on the location and circumstances, if a nonmedical coroner needed an autopsy performed, they might be able to send the body to a medical examiner.

All of this is to say that when it's revealed that Tommy Til-den (played by Brian Cox) is a coroner, that helped me accept that he and his assistant, Austin (also his son, for purposes of narrative tension; played by Emile Hirsch), don't wear masks or hair nets, and are presumably shedding DNA into crime scene evidence on a regular basis. (Masks on actors is an issue, I get it; I can still gripe about the hair.)

As far as the crematorium…I don't know. I guess a funer-al director could just as easily be elected coroner as any other person. At least they're familiar with death, decomp, and basic anatomy. I might feel a little weird about the person in charge of forensic inquests being able to incinerate evidence, though. And to clarify, while I've known many morticians who are true-crime enthusiasts, morticians working in funeral homes do *not* perform autopsies.

The title of coroner here is a load-bearing structure when it comes to my suspension of disbelief, and even that is strained to capacity. When Austin's girlfriend shows up and wants to see a dead body, Dad gives his blessing. Professional ethics? What are those? This allows the audience to catch a glimpse of a couple of corpses in the racks. One of them, a woman who apparently died of cancer, has her *mouth sewn shut.* Like visibly, sutures on the outside of the lips. This is a mutilation lawsuit waiting to happen. Another body was the victim of a gunshot wound to the face. I have to give the special effects designers a pass on this one, but I have repaired those types of injuries, and this one was not remotely realistic. I'm more hung up on the absolute lack of confidentiality for the deceased, and the bizarre mutilation.

The girlfriend is still on the premises when the sheriff arrives with the mystery corpse, asking Tommy to ascertain the cause of death by the next day. Because of the aforementioned family tensions, Austin chooses to stay and help his dad with this pressing autopsy instead of going out with his girlfriend. I would have done the same thing, of course, but we-the-viewer realize he's making a terrible mistake.

I don't mean to be an utter killjoy. The movie does many things well, and the next section is rather engaging. An old funeral home basement with a creaky elevator is a great setting. There's some effective use of diegetic music and radio news, and the overall atmosphere is spooky. I enjoy Brian Cox as an actor in general, and he and Emile Hirsch sell the father/son tension and affection. The slow revelation of just how weird this mysterious woman's corpse is probably works really well for viewers whose hearts aren't wizened coals.

Bits of random trivia: rib shears do come in a range of sizes, but usually you just need the smaller versions—clavicles are harder to cut through; the bone saw made me happy, as did the angle of the cranial incision and the way they pulled the scalp forward; tissue doesn't just peel off the bone like that, though, you have to separate it carefully with instruments. There's a particular foley opportunity they missed for the sound that… husking…the meninges makes when you remove a calvarium. That's a little niche, though, so I give them a pass.

But, speaking of lawsuits… At one point during the mounting tension, the family cat is discovered dying of a gruesome wound. Tommy ends his suffering and…disposes of the body in the retort. The retort used for human remains. No, my friends, no. If this movie had been set in Colorado (a state where the funeral service industry is notoriously unregulated), I would be much happier.

Everything goes downhill from there. For the characters, I mean. Tommy solves the mystery of Jane Doe (which unfortunately lost me all over again plotwise), but too late to save our heroes. The sheriff arrives to once again find people he knew inexplicably and brutally killed, and the once-again unblemished Jane Doe on a table. His response is to ship the body off to Virginia Commonwealth University and their forensic department, which made me cackle. (We got to embalm some cadavers for them recently, and it was awesome!)

A lot of people really like this movie, and I see why. The premise is fun and creepy. I love the idea of the corpse itself being the source of the supernatural shenanigans, since I've never understood why any ghost would haunt a funeral home. The explanation for the haunted corpse, however, leaves me cold. (Sorry.) And as much as I love Brian Cox, someone should have shut that "Morgue and Crematorium" down for ethical violations years ago.

If you have questions—or movie suggestions—for the necromancer, submit them through our portal. In the meantime, I'll be brainstorming what kinds of spooky happenings I can set in a college embalming lab.

Fiction

THE PATH SHE SINGS

Vanesa Fogg

WHEN THE COLD MIST COMES with its needle-fine teeth, you must lie very, very still. You must close your eyes and silence your breath. Empty your mind of everything, save images of darkness. Think of night and rain and worms crawling through earth. The coldness of marble tombs. The breath of ancient sepulchers. Imagine yourself dead. Pretend to be dead. This is the only way to survive.

My wife knew this, just as all in town know. But something happened; she slipped up, the mist got her.

So now I lie in bed alone, pretending to be dead as the bedside candle dies and smokes its last acrid breath. As my dead wife moves restlessly in the kitchen downstairs: opening and shutting drawers, rattling pots and pans, and humming old children's songs out of tune.

———

Like all the dead, Elsie is cold to the touch. Her skin is blue-gray. Her eyes are unfocused; they have the look of the blind.

In our shared house, she glides past me as though I'm not even here. She empties the dresser drawers, then puts everything back; empties them again and puts everything back. She cuts the newspaper into ragged snowflake shapes. She takes rotting vegetables from the fridge and heats them all in a soup that no one drinks. She lies on the living room floor for hours at a time, her eyes open and empty, a lifeless mannequin-doll replica of my wife.

When she speaks, it's in the speech of the dead: senseless, random words strung together. *Star,* she says, her eyes turned to me but not seeing. *Wax, pond, rock. Flutter.*

I know what I must do.

The town council sends me notices, reminding me of my duty. Messages arrive from family and friends, doing the same. All of them urging me toward the deed. Encouragement, advice, and growing concern.

Don't wait, they say. *Get it over with. Only then can you truly grieve.*

Do it now, they say. *Before it's too late.*

You're only making it harder, my brother texts. *More dangerous. You're only hurting yourself.*

No one will visit while Elsie's corpse still walks. But among the warning notices and bills, there are condolence cards and gifts. Casseroles on the doorstep, along with soup and bread. And flowers. Peonies, hydrangea, bouquets of bright lilies. Elsie's favorite flowers. She was loved.

———

Dead-Elsie hums tunelessly as I move about the house. As I heat gifts of food and eat them alone. As I read my instruction guide and repeat its underlined mantra: *It's not her. It's not her.*

Not-Elsie has fished dead flowers from the trash. She wears blue hydrangea petals in her hair. Rotting and bruised. Her blue eyes shine. They were not blue in life.

Silence, she sings in a sweet, familiar voice. *Grass, breath, darkness. Wait for me a while, beloved? Roses are red and violets are blue. We all fall down.*

———

It's not her. The Dead are changed, and they don't come back.

It's not her. Not Elsie, my brown-eyed girl. My sweetheart, a perpetual whirl of motion, busy organizing dinners, parties, food drop-offs for a sick friend. Cooking, gardening, crafting, chatting. Bursting with projects and energy and life.

Not her, not my wife, not the woman who dissolves into giggles like a little girl, reaching to steady herself on my arm. Who puts her cold feet on my legs at night. Who cries over the same movie three times in a row. Who used to sneak out of her house as a kid to meet me under the stars. Elsie, my love. My best friend.

No, she's not this thing in my house now, who wears my wife's face. Silent, save for the songs and cryptic speech of the Dead.

I hold the knife the town council gave me. I watch the light flash off its keen edge.

She's lying on the floor, in one of her motionless spells. It's been minutes since I last saw her move. Her chest neither rises nor falls.

I approach. Her eyes stare blankly upward, like twin blue stars. I've practiced this so many times in my head, just as the instruction guide says. I've watched the videos. I've even practiced on the dummy they sent me—the overhead swing of the arm, the arc of the blade. The point entering precisely where her dead heart beats.

And I can't. My legs are already faltering.

I can't. My arm's trembling. My entire body shakes.

I can't. I back away, and my knees buckle. The knife slips from my hand. Elsie. Acid burns in my throat; I can't breathe. Elsie, Elsie. Forgive me. I'm on the floor, heaving. I can't, I can't, I can't.

It's not Elsie, but her voice is the same. When she stops the tuneless humming, when she lifts her voice in song—it's her. Even as her words are pure nonsense. Her voice is sweet and clear and achingly pure. It sounds like home.

Waters flow west, she sings. *Row, row the boat, my love. Gently, the stream.*

———

The cold mist comes, for the first time since it took my Elsie away. I lock my bedroom door.

This is one of the ways in which keeping the Dead around is dangerous: they might distract you, interrupt you while you're trying to play dead yourself.

The candle on the bedside table flickers. The first warning.

I turn off the overhead light. I lie on the bed like a corpse laid out for a viewing.

Once-Elsie clatters about downstairs; I close my eyes and try to quiet my breathing. To slow my heart. Darkness, darkness. The cold mist is gathering. The temperature plunges. I lie limp, trying to calm my screaming nerves. And now it's here, in my room; it's nibbling at my feet. Its sharp, fine-pointed teeth. The mist creeps slowly up my body, seeking warmth. Needle-brush of teeth against my skin. And now it's unfurling tendrils and wisps of cold, and it's searching, searching. . .

And will he not come again? Dead-Elsie sings downstairs. *Will he not come?*

Her voice is a sweeter strain of darkness in the night. An invitation, an escape. I take it—I follow her voice down and downward, onto a path that winds among ancient sepulchers and gravestones. Under yew trees dripping with rain. The cold earth speaks. I enter the earth, I follow the worms. I flee the creeping mist—I flee Death—into the arms of the Dead.

———

Moth, she sings. *Tremble, flight. Dead, dead, dead.*

———

The weather report calls for fog again tonight. But I haven't locked her out this time. I'm sitting with her on our bed. She's still Elsie. Changed, yes, and strange—all laughter gone. But she's looking at me again. Speaking directly to me. I see my reflection in her eyes.

Don't listen to the songs of the Dead, they all warned.

The candle-flame gutters. I leave the lights on. The cold mist is coming.

I meet it upright, my eyes open. My hand in Elsie's cold hand. *Here,* she tells me. *Stone, pupae, breaking. Come.* She smiles. Her blue eyes shine. And I follow her, my guide and my bride, into the gathering mist.

THE LANGUAGE OF FIREFLIES

Angela Liu

The streets are lined with glass trees
We weave through their false light
      for a taste of a real moon, fold

secrets into telescope wings
where utopia is reachable
      if you slumber for another million years.

At dusk, we follow bodies
like burning arrowheads, play
witnesses to every nightly procession,
      every rainy wedding of the foxes.

We ping desire into the summer wind,
the lusty curtain of charcoal smoke, our bodies
      heavy with want, stopping

on a leaf, a windowsill, a neon half-moon
under a club awning
We are the emerald necklace of light
      laced around summer night.

Cloaked in autumn gold,
we cling to dried stalks, mouthless,
      longing for home through a growing silver fog

Extinction is a dream
where we finally find a winter moon
to call our own
      a paradise of spilling stars.

SAINT GREMMY

Robert Nazar Arjoyan

THAT FIRST PEARL falls from an iron sky glowing orange, the lights of L.A. unable to break through the thick bulwark, and this perfect teardrop dives from the clouds to remind an old woman of her single, lonesome secret.

Gremmy loves to drive in the rain.

She lowers the volume of her radio sermon to better hear the pit-a-pat of those swelling sprinkles and their pleasing arrhythmia, a more unblunted homily from God straight above.

Gremmy has little use for secrets, let alone room for them. Secrets demand space, secrets entail interiority, and in their quiet way, secrets turn a human into a person. But as busy as Gremmy is, was, and will be, secrets are simply impossible. Daughter, then bride, then mother, then grandmother. When one is needed like Gremmy is needed, it's very easy to be all those things but extremely difficult to be yourself. So whenever the Lord deems fit, she celebrates this one treasure of herself.

Gremmy loves to drive in the rain.

She also loves her grandson Ricky, and that is no secret, not at all.

Gremmy goes east toward the boy's high school while the trickle fattens into a torrent. She cracks her window an inch or two and allows the water to stipple the sleeve of her cardigan. To anoint her gnarled knuckles twisted by time and cracked with care.

The saint of our family, Ricky often says.

He had asked Gremmy to attend his play tonight, alone, and she giggled because naturally that was a given. Dates were few and far between for Gremmy. But Ricky didn't meet her glee when he said he had something he wanted to tell her.

Needed to tell her. Gremmy had ever been Ricky's confidante, from his first confession in kindergarten about eating crayons to just last week when Ricky cheated on an exam, and Gremmy would not fail him now.

So on she drives in the rain.

The strengthening shower in her Toyota's headlights reminds Gremmy of awful Armenia, fireflies winking in nighttime's gloom while she pinned sheets in a chill wind. Gremmy would prefer laundry to dry in this manner still, but her schedule won't allow it. Her own home, her son's, her bootless husband, her overactive grandchildren. By now she knows all of their secrets, legible in diet and dirty underwear alike.

Gremmy changes lanes as she nears the campus, back for her second time that day. Well, who else picks up Ricky? Oh, but these commutes she so cherishes, minutes alone with her chosen dearest. She grins unaware while merging, but her tires slip and scuttle across the skin of water. Gremmy restores the sedan without issue and checks her mirrors to make sure—

A hearse.

Gremmy gasps, crow's feet diminished by virtue of her electrified eyes locked on the rearview wherefrom swings a Christ crucified.

A hearse indeed trails behind, closer, seemingly overtaken by Gremmy. Her stare darts back and forth from the road to the hearse, from the road to the hearse, from the road to the hearse. Woodleigh Lane, there trailing, Gould Avenue, shadowing yet, the hard rain now a curtain pulled apart by her wrenching wipers to briefly reveal the black-and-grey car.

Gremmy blows past Georgia Road beneath a green light.

The grill of the hearse appears to her as a smile, but one such reserved for the wicked, those abrim with sin.

Crown Avenue flies by under a cautionary yellow.

Its upraised roof is a monstrous hunch, some tumorous burden pressing down on an eager ogre. Gremmy wonders if the hearse is occupied when a volley of honks clutches her waning attention.

She blinks into the immediate present of Daleridge Road only to see a red traffic light drift over her Toyota and hear the screeching of vehicles sliding on either side. That hostile red light burns a brand upon her retinas, usurps Gremmy's whole horizon when all she wants to see is Ricky, and—and then she's on the other side.

"Thank God, oh, *park kez Ter Astvats*," she says.

Gremmy rips her foot off the gas and coasts, willing the clean rain to purify her humors, at once polluted by a churn of adrenaline and fear. She breathes and breathes again, and the hammer inside her chest relaxes while the flow of travel behind her commences.

Gremmy chances another look in the rearview and witnesses the hearse going right at the intersection she narrowly escaped.

She enters the parking lot of Saint Francis High School and pulls her Toyota into a vacancy ensconced by the halo of a foggy lamppost. The spots are almost entirely full, families filing in for a night of drama. The muffled laughter of the young penetrates the quiet of the parking lot, the synchronous scuffing of sneakers like hysterical violins. This is the last performance of the season, Ricky's final time on stage before graduation, his first starring role. Gremmy can't recall the name of the production just then, but it's that movie with Jack something-or-other when he screams in a courtroom about handling the truth. Ricky is playing the young lawyer, the man from all those spy movies and the Hollywood religion.

Gremmy's life hasn't been hers for half a century plus, but she thanks God for bringing her here in the rain, and for bringing Ricky to her. It was just last Thanksgiving when the boy stood and read a speech about their relationship. *You're my best friend, Gremmy*, Ricky said.

No one had called her that before.

Gremmy nudges open the door with a wobbly knee and hoists herself upward while wielding an umbrella, because even though she loves to drive in the rain, she hates to walk in it. Puddles rise to meet her tread as Gremmy goes to the quad of Saint Francis. Crossing the drop-off area, her feet stutter as the hearse bobs across a speed bump and blinds Gremmy with its shining glare. But as the offending high beams retreat, so too does her instant panic. Nothing more than an ordinary Lincoln Town Car, the selfsame hunk of junk her husband drove back in his more ambulatory days.

The rain has wasted to mist, so Gremmy sheathes her umbrella. Her glasses are water-dotted, but she can still see the statue of Saint Francis tending his animals, sees him well. Gremmy bends her neck in his direction before entering a lavish plaza done in the Mediterranean mode.

Peace blankets her here within this vicarious experience of community and camaraderie. Olive trees and succulents and riotous flowers color the courtyard, white stanchions of a football field like sentries in the far distance. Ricky's older brother broke his clavicle under those posts not three years ago, that fool, the white of his jutted bone ablaze in their gleam. Gremmy strolls tutting as final raindrops touch her face, an isolate being for the moment unobliged, for the moment unnoticed.

Tables providing coffee and cookies and candy are propped end to end under a vine-gripped arcade, parents pitching in their share. Gremmy recognizes so many of them. She winds her way through the mingling mothers and fraternizing fathers, eager for some caffeine to settle her jangled nerves and maybe even an indulgence of sweets.

Like her faith, Gremmy's English is perfect, tiny accent aside.

"Hello," says she. "May I please have a cup of black coffee? And an oatmeal co—"

The woman sitting opposite Gremmy looks up, and her mask of greeting ruptures into naked horror. This woman shrieks before clapping mute her stretched mouth.

"Are you all right, miss?" seeks Gremmy, leaning closer, but the woman shoots out her hand and locks Gremmy's wrist like a cuff to arrest her advance, and born of their unforeseen union Gremmy knows, simply knows, that this person kicks the family cat when no one else is home, that she steps on its nape and releases, steps and releases, like she's tapping along to the beat of her favorite song.

Gremmy knows her secret.

But before she can parse this bizarrity, the woman recoils, blond and prim, with chemical lips, her spine pushing her chair and making it whine through the air.

"Miss, w—"

"I'm sorry, ma'am, I'm sorry," interrupts the woman. "It's your eyes."

"My eyes?"

The woman physically turns away before responding with a nod of her trembling head.

"My eyes?" Gremmy asks again. She'd checked her appearance in the bathroom mirror prior to departing but not before exiting the Toyota. She isn't vain, she's aware of her looks. Besides, Ricky has told Gremmy for as long as he could talk that she resembles Robin Williams.

Gremmy blinks with searching intent but nothing feels off, no ocular pain or skewed sight. The crowd leers at her askance, and their flanking whispers sand Gremmy's blushed ears. Whatever vapor dewed the lines of her cheeks a minute ago evaporates at this mortification. Gremmy grinds her dentures, a creak like ragged leather loud in her skull.

"Someone just give her the coffee already," spits the woman, still avoiding any sort of directness. "And the cat," she continues with even more pronounced reticence. "He's fine."

Irrespective of the strange circumstance, Gremmy knows a lie when she hears a lie. Her eyes might be compromised, but her ears are expert.

Gremmy snatches her goods and stalks to the center of the courtyard, where a fountain warbles to itself, just as Gremmy does. She senses the edgy undertones of the crowd behind her, Gremmy so scarred by backflung barbs yet pricked by them still. She plants herself on a large rock, another sculpture of

Saint Francis looming over his animals. His shadow capes her stooped shoulders, and all the mountains beyond the football field are shapes without detail, shapes without detail.

Gremmy sips her acrid coffee and then pours the remains into the water. She scoots around and peers into the pool, where in the placid surface Gremmy understands the mass agitation, though it affords her no comfort.

Her eyes, the right and the left, are changed.

"Jesus have mercy," says her reflection.

Where once there was white there is now only red, a great spill of blood flooding the sclera.

"Jesus have mercy," says Gremmy, and springs up so fast that her neck locks in place as if each tendon is trapped between sharp vertebrae. Gremmy always wakes at 4:00 a.m. to pray, thanking God for a new day with her first thought before she thinks of any other. Maybe this is her body's unsubtle intervention, hemorrhages and spasms, its way of telling her to relax, to slow down, to stop being everything for everyone.

Maybe it is God's divine intercession.

Three sonorous chimes echo across the expanse of the courtyard as lamps begin to dim. The figure of Saint Francis remains lit, however, illumination from the small pond dancing like upset mercury on his carved features. Gremmy stands and notices a fox at the feet of the saint. Turquoise from snout to tail, with streaks of rust scoring the body. She waits for an invasion of scarlet, for her eyes to burst and bleed, but everything remains earthly, her vision unhampered by a crimson hell.

"Good night," she says to Saint Francis and his fox as the crowd shuffles toward the theatre. Gremmy too joins the throng, her head down and her pace sedate. Ricky got her a seat in the front row, better for her to see but also convenient should she need to leave. *If Papik or Dad or Noah need you,* Ricky said.

No, Ricky, tonight you are my one and only.

She said that to him with the certainty of a sunrise.

Gremmy finds her seat and eases into the plush backing. The stage is impeccable, professional, a foreboding bench abutted by two witness stands, and Gremmy marvels at the school's expense. The house fills in minutes, the chairs on either side of her in seconds. The man to her left stops in a squat, and Gremmy is certain why so she spares him by averting her stained eyes. When he finally does sit, the arm of his suede jacket touches Gremmy's pinky finger, and she knows that his jacket is stolen.

The man's nostrils flare as he bothers his wedding ring.

"I have two sons here and a daughter at Sacred Heart..."

Gremmy listens.

"Every penny is for them, and that's fine. That's the way it's supposed to be. I just, all the parents drive luxury cars and wear designer clothes..."

Gremmy nods.

"I don't want my children left out. And I don't want them to hate me, so." He smooths the lapel of his jacket. "You understand."

"Yes."

The man knuckles back tears.

"Thank you."

Perhaps the hemorrhage is worse than Gremmy thinks if she's conjuring kicked cats and stolen clothes. Some insidious stroke. Maybe she should call her son, but no, he's probably out drinking someplace. How about Noah? Gallivanting on his motorcycle without a helmet, that idiot. And what of her husband? Doubtless asleep in his bed, Gremmy's own bed waiting made and warm. How sleepy she is, sleepier still as the lights go down and the actors assume their places.

Gremmy blinks to stay awake, but her eyelids grow heavier with successive flutters. It's only when she hears Ricky's voice, the voice she's heard descend from squeaky to strong, that she rouses.

He strides on stage, a smirk crowning his chin and pointing to the keen corners of his jaw. The crisp white shirt strains against his water polo chest, tanned hands lazy in his pockets. Her handsome boy!

Ricky delivers his lines and sits at a table and while his scene partner speaks, Ricky's gaze lands on Gremmy. His face sags, lips parting of their own volition. Her eyes to him must look like a pair of Christmas ornaments glinting in the dark, familiar but frightful. Ever so slightly, Ricky cocks his head upward, an inquiry of reassurance learned at Gremmy's lap. She sends him the same gesture, her answer, and Ricky picks up where he left off without missing his cue.

Lethargy comes and goes in waves as the play progresses, at times coddling Gremmy while at others thrashing her, and before long, the lights fade up and someone somewhere announces intermission. She stays put while the audience exits, thinking about whether she should linger or leave. The last thing she wants is to get into another near miss while driving. So Gremmy hauls herself up.

"Gremmy!"

Ricky's head floats from behind a side door.

"You came!"

"Of course I did. Nothing could stop me from seeing you."

"You're a saint. Hey, how do you say 'saint' in Armenian again?"

She huffs through her nose.

"*Soorp.*"

"Right, *soorp*. You're a *soorp*, Gremmy."

She laughs, and he clears his throat.

"Is it good? The play, I mean."

"Very good, *balas*. You are wonderful."

He regards her sanguine eyes again, squints.

"And are you sure you're okay?"

Gremmy nods. Ricky's head looks backstage, listening.

"Gotta go, Gremmy."

"Ricky, wasn't there something you wanted to tell me?"

"Umm…"

One of Gremmy's kneecaps slides out of true while she stands by.

"Can it wait?" he asks her.

"Can it?" she asks him.

Ricky rubs the nape of his neck.

"I really have to go, Gremmy."

Gremmy's kneecap pops back in place, as does unexpected relief.

"Okay, *hokees*, go."

Ricky smiles at Gremmy and she sees the toddler he was, the man he will someday be. Whatever happened to her eyes, this panoramic perception is crystal clear, and for that she again thanks God. Suddenly, Ricky toes the dropdown door holder and jogs to Gremmy, his rangy legs conveying him in five nonchalant strides. He envelops her in a hug, and between the heat of his biceps, Gremmy now knows his secret.

Does it disappoint her? She'd be lying if she said no.

Does she love Ricky any less? She'd be lying if she said yes.

His abrupt inhalation shivers her very soul.

"Gremmy, I—"

"Shh. You don't have to tell me anything."

She holds him out at arm's length, her thumbs kneading his wide shoulders.

"You used to fit right in my elbow, Ricky."

"Now you can probably fit in mine."

They chuckle, but the sound is new.

"I love you, okay? I promise I love you."

And his lips are a dam, but his head rocks up and down. Gremmy feels his anguish and wants to take it from him.

"Have a great play, Ricky."

"Wha—Are you leaving?"

"Maybe I go check on Papik, huh? You know how he is."

"Gremmy, don't go just because—"

"You're beautiful up there. I know you will do great."

From the wings a voice calls out for Ricky to hurry up already.

"Thanks, Gremmy."

"For what, *jana*?"

The boy blows her a kiss and lopes back to his life.

Gremmy walks up the aisle and through the foyer, awash in confusion. Her willingness to give Ricky the space he needs far outweighs her selfish desire to stay and unwillingly smother it.

Outside, the clouds have cleared to reveal the few scant stars permitted to dress the skies of Los Angeles. A thick crowd clutters the entrance of the theatre, in the direction of the parking lot. Not wishing to experience anyone else's inner world, Gremmy circumvents the loitering horde and straight-away understands their thralldom.

There in the center of the roundabout sits a fox on its haunches. The critter spies Gremmy and yaps, its fuzzy head pointed right at her. Gremmy remains motionless as the throng observes. The fox yaps again, shriller, urgent, and impatiently hops to, sashaying its fiery fur. Gremmy glances at the crowd, these people she's circled for years, and they flinch as one.

Grace visits Gremmy again this night as it did hours ago with the rain, sudden and swift. Cloistered together, she and they, a lifting of the veil occurs, the drawing of some giant drapery with Gremmy spotlit, a confidence shared among themselves. They glimpse this enigma of all and everything, the impregnable mystery up close, and know.

The fox yaps a third time, angling its smallish head at Gremmy. She turns on her heel and follows the beast as three chimes from behind indicate resumption for everyone else.

Upstairs they climb, the fox's claws clicking atop the pavement and echoing around the concrete pylons. Swishing back and forth as would a metronome, its vulpine tail a lure leading Gremmy to her level, where she turns the corner and freezes.

Within the halo of the lamppost where her Toyota should be parked idles the hearse, doused in a color of honey. The fox carries on apace toward the vehicle as Gremmy remains fixed, and the open air surrounding her suddenly slams tight like the lid of a jar. Awful Armenia steals Gremmy's memory once more, their breathless cellar packed with preserves, and the driver's door of the hearse mewls open. Gremmy wishes she had stayed to watch the rest of Ricky's play. One bare foot followed by the other steps out of the hearse and lights upon the still wet cement. The bottom half of a brown tunic skirts the ground as Saint Francis unfurls from the hearse and stands to his full height. The fox settles down beside him and pants with a contented tongue, and it's so similar to the courtyard statue that Gremmy considers jumping off the roof.

Saint Francis extends his emaciated hand to her, his flesh a prime example of poverty's vow. Gremmy contemplates how Ricky will get home, how her husband will have breakfast tomorrow, if her son and Noah will someday murder each other. Even now, in this hour, she prays for them.

The hearse's engine purrs to life.

As Saint Francis glides to Gremmy, she tries to pinpoint precisely when she died and decides it must have been at the red light.

Nearer now he sails, and from his robes she whiffs the assaultive stench of barns, hay, fur, feed, and good Lord of course it's Saint Francis who shall escort Gremmy deep into the blue hereafter, this steward of animals, of course it is. Butterflies billow free from his sleeves as Saint Francis rests the tips of his withered fingers just so on Gremmy's forehead and rain falls from a singing sky to bless her journey. He opens the door and helps her in, but of course he does.

"After all," Gremmy says to him, "we're just animals, aren't we?"

Animals with secrets.

And the hearse moves in no discernible direction with Francis at the wheel and his fox curled at Gremmy's feet. Above the din of heaven's rain, she can hear applause clamorous like thunder. For Ricky? No.

For her.

For Saint Gremmy.

Poetry

THINGS FOR WHICH I HAVE NOT ASCERTAINED YOUR CONSENT

RB Lemberg

for Corey

1. TRAVELING TO THE UNDERWORLD TO RETRIEVE YOU

I do not know if you are there, but the whole romantic notion
of a journey, a boat, a coin,
a hooded stranger—where were they all
when you lay there slipping downriver
without a boat or a coin to pay for it—
where were they all? Where was I? What kind of coin
would I need, to cross and to come back,
let alone ask for your permission?

2. GRIEVING YOU

A sound ceases. It was
an elaborate, persistent sound
both gentle and cutting, heard
by those of us who notice every rustle—
the hum of the refrigerator, the creak of a tree,
an unseen passing of a possum by the storm door,
the sigh of stars that keep on traveling the night sky
ten thousand light-years after death—
and then, like a thirst quenched without asking—your voice;
when it ceased, we were bereft
but the world kept on and kept on.

Do I even have
your permission to speak of this? Do the dead

consent to the grief of the living? What if
it's a burden? A violation?

3. ASKING THE SEPHIROT ABOUT MIRACLES

In a world where all suffering is made soft
between the hands of Chesed,
I wonder if miracles are allowed to exist.
I was taught that the dead are ghosts, the dead
are dybbuks that cling to the living
to be purified by virtue—but I think
it's in reverse:
the living are dybbuks that cling to the dead,
the living are ghosts that haunt and haunt the places
where death could be untruthed; an imprint, a grief-haunting
that can be cleansed by holy melody
that ascends from violins and clarinets
and drums and cymbals and an electric guitar and the wail
of our stories, virtue be damned,
the song that soars us past our mythologies
into a life-death where we can simply be,
where we can simply
share book recommendations
simply
read each other's stories, simply say
"Please rest,"
but there's no melody like this. No miracle.
No rebbe.

4. SAYING KADDISH

Magnified and sanctified be Their holy name—
but which one? We trans folk often
have many names, and G-d certainly
qualified a thousand times over,
creating us all in Their image. G-d created

for six days without resting, but not a single time an underworld
or heaven, or a purgatory:

no, They let us live.
We, on our own, have learned to haunt each other,
to change each other,
burrow deep into the shadows of each other,
write books, and share them with each other,
and lose the files, and die without a will,
and know the deep and dark and sideways of each other,
and say the words
beyond the breath.

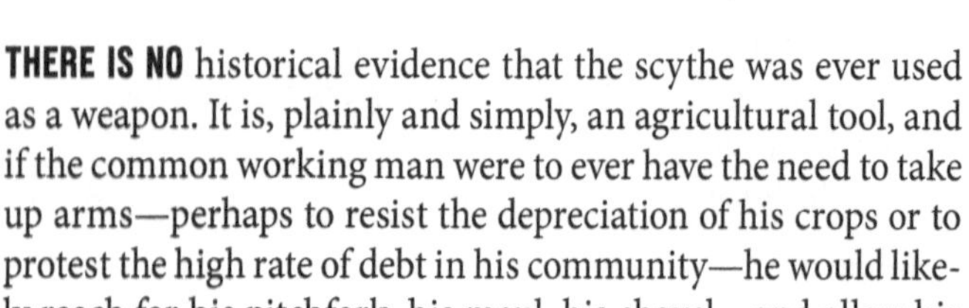

THE SCYTHE AND OTHER SIMPLE MECHANISMS

T.E.Z. Moore

THERE IS NO historical evidence that the scythe was ever used as a weapon. It is, plainly and simply, an agricultural tool, and if the common working man were to ever have the need to take up arms—perhaps to resist the depreciation of his crops or to protest the high rate of debt in his community—he would likely reach for his pitchfork, his maul, his shovel—and allow his scythe, its blade worn and dulled from stray pebble and sand, to sit peacefully in the back shed.

If you look out, beyond and over the hill, you will see a Farmer in the field. The Farmer is not always in the field—there are many other working parts on a Farm that need attending to—but today it is a dense fall morning and the dew will cling long to the quivering stalks of the Farmer's ripe crop, past the sun's rising and well into its eastern arc, and so today the Farmer is in the field, because a scythe cuts best when the grass is wet.

That is not to say that this particular scythe, in the palms of this particular Farmer, would have much trouble in weather drier than now. Perhaps a split end here or there, the beginnings of wear on the blade, metal easily shepherded back into alignment by the Farmer's keen whetstone, fine-but-not-too-fine-grind, the best and most loyal friend of any steel that yearns for sharpness. This scythe is long-bladed and razor-edged—a testament to the Farmer's honed knowledge and skill. It will not be deterred by a mere drop in humidity.

Still, part of caring for one's tools is allowing them to work in ideal conditions. The Scythe does not need to be tested to its limit, constantly pushing the boundaries of scytheness. It only needs to reap the crop.

The process is simple. A short step into the swathe. Steady grip on the handles and a planting of the feet. Then—arms sweep, an artful curve from hip to spine, as if the body were enshrouded in steam and slowly bent by two hands. Across, follow through. Let the weight of the blade do the work.

Scht.

And again.

Scht.

And again.

Scht.

July 6, 1685. James Scott, 1st Duke of Monmouth, leads 5,000 peasant-soldiers to battle against the English Army in an attempt to overthrow his uncle, King James II. They are armed with 5,000 straight-handled polearms, at the ends of which sit 5,000 curved blades—cutting edge, concave. A so-called "war-scythe" can no longer harvest grain, or mow grass, or do much of anything a scythe might be wont to do. The blade has been separated from the snath, thrown in the fire and reforged, re-fitted. The tang has been strengthened with extraneous rods and bolts, and the entire head has been twisted a full ninety degrees so that the tip points outward, can slide into a stomach easier than a stalk. The peasants lose desperately, and it takes several swings of the ax before the Duke's head knocks loose.

One of the most important aspects of scythe maintenance is the sharpening of the blade. The Farmer keeps a small, water-filled sheath at their hip, in which the whetstone sits, never more than a quickdraw away. The Farmer reaches for it now, stands the Scythe on its upper grip so that the blade—wet, spattered with plant matter—hangs long and looming. The detritus is easily wiped away by the sunwarm cotton of the Farmer's sleeve.

It's best to start on the side of the scythe facing away from you so that, in the case of a lingering burr, the sharp flap will point up toward the grass, and not down toward the soil. The Farmer is always very certain to remove the burr in its entirety with a single, practiced swipe of the whetstone, and so they have not made this mistake in a very long time, but every master was once a beginner, and so the Farmer starts on the inside of the blade.

One stroke on the left, stone against spine, and then an equal stroke on the right. In bits like this, all down the length of the blade. Just a few times over is enough. In fifteen minutes, the Farmer will stop and repeat this process, so that there is never a single moment when the blade is dull. Tomorrow morning, before the sun rises, the Farmer and Scythe will settle at the anvil and peen yesterday's wear from the blade—the sharp *plink* of the hammer, the dawn's first birdsong.

The Farmer brushes their thumb across the blade and deems it sharp enough. Back on the ground, amongst the crop, the soft metal reflects a ghostly blue. Ghosts are always blue, aren't they? In the same way that the plague is black and the whale is white and the Scythe is long and looming. Some type of truth that is not a reality.

Scht, scht, scht.

Just like that, the stalks are severed clean through, their blue light fading as they fall, gently, the laying of a head on a warm pillow. The Scythe guides them to the windrow, where they will rest until the field is done, waiting patiently to be threshed with the Farmer's flail. The threshing will be hard and heaving, but the fruit must be knocked loose so that the grain can be properly harvested, so that the empty stalks may relax into new soil, ready to fertilize a future crop.

The Farmer wipes the sweat from their brow and replants the woven hat on their head. A flail, yes, that could do some damage. Have you ever seen Death brandish a flail? No? How odd. It is very difficult to hurt yourself with a scythe. The snath is much too long, and the point of the blade is huddled down and away. Is it sharpness that people find so frightening? Curvature? Or is it simply the process of reaping? The moment that one stalk is severed from the rest?

———

George Washington is not a wheat farmer. He piles the tasks that would make him so onto the heads and backs and necks and arms and shoulders and legs of the people he keeps imprisoned at Mount Vernon. Washington arms them with scythes at the harvest and expects to reap the fruits of their labor.

It is very important that wheat is harvested in a timely manner. The berries are only ripe for so long, and the crows and the winds will have them even before they soften. Mount Vernon's reapers set out in a team, scythes in hand, and make the decision to work as slowly as possible, like scientists held hostage, sabotaging in small ways the world-ending weapons they are forced to create. They ding their blades on rocks, twist their ankles in the field, wield their false incompetence like it is hot and iron, know that it will fold into the finest of steel. Washington does not notice, because he believes he is a wheat farmer. He will not notice until the day his throat grows sore and tired.

Scht, scht, scht.

Even once the threshing is done, soul-grain can be tricky to winnow. Its chaff is heavy and it clings to the fruit, stubborn, through even harsh winds. The seeds are small—rough, but fragile—and they cannot easily roll themselves down the slant of a cookie tin, leaving the chaff behind. And so the Farmer must attend to the grain by hand. Just a few at a time, to rub against the callouses and crevices of their palms, careful not to crack.

Here, a hare, cut and shredded by large talons and hawk chick mouths. A human, old, with a UTI that has spread to the kidneys. A human, young, caught beneath the rumble of a bulldozer. A great tree, felled after two hundred years, and with it the host of lives it sheltered. They run through the Farmer's fingers and into the sieve, where the loosened chaff can catch in the Farmer's cool breath, carry off and collect as dust bunnies in the shed, as all things eventually do.

For now, though, the Farmer is in the field, and it has begun to rain. It is not so much at first, but soon the swath is sludgy and slick, and the Scythe's chine cakes with mud. The Farmer sighs, unsticks their sinking boot with a *pop*, untangles the Scythe from the stalks, and finds, in the curve of the blade, a freshly-cut seed head, still thrumming with a quiet light. As one would do with any infant, the Farmer gently lifts its cradle and shields it from the pouring rain.

KATE LECHLER'S work has appeared in *Shimmer Magazine, Pod-Castle, Fireside Fiction,* and previously here in *The Deadlands,* among other places. Kate lives in Chicago with their good dog Charlie, and teaches first-year writing for the School of the Art Institute of Chicago. When they are not working on a novella about sexy vampire-pirates, there's a good chance you'll find them making magical collages or foraging in the woods of Cook County.

ZAYNAB ILIYASU BOBI, Frontier I, is a Nigerian-Hausa poet, artist, and licensed Medical Laboratory Scientist from Bobi. She is the winner of the 2023 Derricotte/Eady Chapbook Prize and author of *Cadaver of Red Roses* (O, Miami Books) and *Uncensored Snapshots,* forthcoming with Chestnut Review in 2025.

While being rained on adjacent to Portland, Oregon, **MONTE LIN** edits, writes, and plays tabletop roleplaying games and writes short stories. Clarion West got him to write about dying universes, edible sins, dreaming mountains, and singularities made of anxieties. His stories have been published in *Cossmass Infinities, Cast of Wonders,* Flame Tree Press anthologies, and others. His nonfiction has been published at *Strange Horizons.* He is Managing Editor of *Uncanny Magazine* and Staff Editor of Angry Hamster Press. He can be found posting *Doctor Who* news, Asian American diaspora discourse, and his board game losses on Bluesky @montelin.bsky.social.

AARON KNUCKEY lives and writes in the never-ending cornfields of Central Illinois. He has never seen a ghost but one starry night in junior high, he mistook a meteor's blue trail for a UFO, and ever since he has striven to mistake the mundane for the magical (when possible).

CRESSIDA BLAKE ROE is a biracial writer whose work appears in *Lightspeed, The Deadlands, Gamut, Factor Four,* and other venues. Recent stories have been selected for the Wigleaf Top 50 and nominated for the Best Small Fictions. See more at www.cblakeroe.wordpress.com.

VANESSA FOGG dreams of selkies, dragons, and gritty cyberpunk futures from her home in western Michigan. Her writing has appeared in *Lightspeed, Podcastle, GigaNotoSaurus,* Neil Clarke's *The Best Science Fiction of the Year* Vol 4, and the Bram Stoker Award–nominated anthology *Unquiet Spirits: Essays by Asian Women in Horror.* Her debut collection, *The House of Illusionists and Other Stories,* is forthcoming from Interstellar Flight Press. For a complete bibliography and more, visit her website at www.vanessafogg.com.

ANGELA LIU is a Nebula-, Ignyte-, and Rhysling-nominated writer/poet from NYC who writes about intergenerational trauma and weird things. She formerly researched mixed reality storytelling at Keio University in Japan. Her stories and poetry are published in *Strange Horizons, Clarkesworld, The Dark, Interzone Digital, Uncanny, Lightspeed, khōréō,* and *Logic(s),* among others. Check out more of her work at liu-angela.com or find her on Twitter/Instagram @liu_angela and on Bluesky @angelaliu.bsky.social.

ROBERT NAZAR ARJOYAN was born into the Armenian diaspora of Los Angeles. Aside from an arguably ill-advised foray into rock-n-roll bandery during his late teens, literature and movies were the vying forces of his life. Naz graduated from USC's School of Cinematic Arts and now works as an author and filmmaker. When he isn't writing, Naz is likely couchbound with a good book, jamming with his fantastic son, gutbust laughing with his wife/best friend, or farting around in the garden with his purple clippers. You can read his stories in *Maudlin House, Bullshit Lit, Ghoulish Tales, The Deadlands, Cleaver Magazine, Roi Fainéant, Apocalypse Confidential, JMWW, Gone Lawn, The Hooghly Review,* and *River Styx,* with more besides and on the way. Find him at www.arjoyan.com or on socials @RobertArjoyan.

RB LEMBERG (they/them) is a queer, bigender immigrant from Ukraine to the US. RB is an author of six books of speculative fiction and poetry, an academic, and a translator from Ukrainian and Russian. RB's work has been shortlisted for the Le Guin Prize for Fiction, Nebula, Locus, Ignyte, World Fantasy, and other awards. You can find RB on Instagram at @rblemberg, Bluesky at @rblemberg.bsky.social, and at their website rblemberg.net.

T.E.Z. MOORE (they/them) is a queer writer and farmhand from Lancaster, Pennsylvania. They wrote their piece, "The Scythe and Other Simple Mechanisms," out of a growing irritation at scythe-wielding fantasy RPG characters, a transitive love for hand tools, and a firm belief that poetry is inherent in human history. This is their first publication.

STAFF BIOS

SEAN MARKEY publishes websites for a living and has always dreamed of publishing a magazine (about Death). He lives with his wife, Beth, in an old central Vermont farmhouse. Follow Sean on Twitter @PsychopompCom (if you want).

E. CATHERINE TOBLER is a writer and editor. You might know her editing work from *Shimmer Magazine*. You might know her writing from *Clarkesworld, Lightspeed,* and *Apex Magazine*. A trebuchet and Oxford comma enthusiast, she enjoys gelato and beer in her free time. Leo sun, Taurus moon. You can find her on Bluesky @ect.bsky.social.

NICASIO ANDRES REED is a writer, poet, and essayist whose work has appeared in venues such as *Shimmer, Fireside, Lightspeed,* and *Uncanny Magazine*. He's read slush for *Strange Horizons*, edited manuscripts for award-winning authors, and owns five different copies of *Moby Dick*. He lives with his family in Cavite province in the Philippines.

INKSHARK is a scandalously queer illustrator, author, and editor who lives in the rainy wilds of the Pacific Northwest. He enjoys exploring with his dogs, writing impossible things, and painting what he shouldn't. When his current meatshell begins to decay, he'd like science to put his brain into a giant killer octopus body with which he promises to be responsible and not even slightly shipwrecky. Pinky swear.

DAVID GILMORE is a writer, reader, and editor out of St. Louis, MO. His work has been featured in *The Rumpus* and at Lindenwood University, where he also received his MFA. He lives with his wife and son and spends his free time manning a stall in the Goblin Market selling directions to various Underworlds in exchange for rumors and information on where he can find his muse.

AMANDA DOWNUM is the author of *The Necromancer Chronicles, Dreams of Shreds & Tatters,* and the World Fantasy Award–nominated collection *Still So Strange.* Not content with armchair necromancy, she is also a licensed mortician. She lives in Austin, TX, with an invisible cat. You can summon her at a crossroads at midnight on the night of a new moon, or find her on Twitter as @stillsostrange.

LAURA BLACKWELL is a freelance editor and Pushcart-nominated writer. Her publications include *Chiral Mad 5, Nightmare,* and the *Aseptic and Faintly Sadistic* anthology. You can follow her on Bluesky, Instagram, and Twitter @pronouncedlahra and visit her website at pronouncedlahra.com.

CHRISTINE M. SCOTT has been a professional graphic designer, website developer, and brand consultant for more than twenty-five years. She is the creative director and copublisher of Nosetouch Press and has coedited seven anthologies, including the folk horror anthology trilogy *The Fiends in the Furrows.* She is also an artist and craftsperson—several of her handcrafted items were included in *Game of Thrones: The Compendium,* printed by Chronicle Books for HBO. For a complete list of her pursuits, please visit christinemariescott.com.

FELICIA MARTÍNEZ is a writer and artist born and raised in Eastern New Mexico, though home is now the San Francisco Bay Area. She is a 2023 Dream Foundry Contest for Emerging Writers finalist, an honor she achieved with a beloved work of flash. Find her on Bluesky and Instagram as @feliciafm.

ANNIKA BARRANTI KLEIN is a freelance editor with a writing habit. Her work can be found at annikaobscura.com. She is supervised by a cat at all times.

www.ingramcontent.com/pod-product-compliance
Lightning Source LLC
Chambersburg PA
CBHW030947310726
48969CB00008B/2397